The
Flights
of
Marceau

Imagination is a wonderful place to visit!

The Flights of Marceau

BY
JOE BROWN

PAINTINGS BY MICHAEL PUKÁČ

DRAWINGS BY STEPHEN MARCHESI

MAJESTIC EAGLE PUBLISHING CO.
CHICAGO, ILLINOIS

Published by
Majestic Eagle Publishing Co.
6649 Navajo
Lincolnwood, IL 60712

First Edition.

Printed in Canada.

Library of Congress Cataloging in Publication Data
Joe Brown, 1935–
The Flights of Marceau–Week Two

ISBN 978-0-9797495-1-3

www.TheFlightsofMarceau.com

DESIGNED BY MARY KORNBLUM, CMYK DESIGN INC.
PRODUCED BY DELLA R. MANCUSO, MANCUSO ASSOCIATES INC.

To the parents of my thirteen grandchildren
for providing my co-authors:
Dylan, Cody, Jessie,
Jake, Zack, Sam, C.J., Maxx,
Gabe, Duke, Ross, Sloan,
and Sydney.

A new and completely original superhero

Marceau is a New York City taxi driver who, in order to escape from his less than exciting existence, imagines himself participating in amazing, visual adventures which he shares with a regular passenger he drives to and from his office each weekday.

He uses everyday, adult language, to improve the reader's word recognition and vocabulary. An easy, convenient glossary with simple definitions just to the right of the new words is included.

Collaborators in Marceau's quest to "do good" include animals, birds and other living (or not) creatures, the clouds, the sun, the wind and anything else his fertile mind can imagine.

And it is all in rhyme.

Each adventure is short and exciting, to hold the reader's attention. When the story is over, the reader will not only have gained new words, but will understand them in context as well. The tales are entertaining and educational, occasionally focusing on worldly concerns such as global warming and rain-forest awareness.

The good guys always win, the bad guys always lose, and nobody ever gets hurt.

Contents

Marceau Is My Name...

And this is my tale:

I've traveled the seas on the back of a whale
I've flown the sky on butterfly wings
And done many other incredible things.   Incredible = amazing
I've been with an eagle to visit her nest
I've ridden a dolphin high over a crest   Crest = top of a wave
An elephant herd awaits my command
And an eighteen-foot python ate out of my hand.   Python = snake
The clouds have been coaches pulled by the stars
I've visited Venus and Pluto and Mars.
I've cured many ills, I've wished away warts
I'm the undisputed champion of physical sports.   Undisputed = agreed

So, Marceau is my name and I'm driving a cab
And my mind does me proud to escape from the drab.   Drab = dreary
For the world as I know it is tired and dry
But my mind lets me leap to the heights of the sky.   Heights = top

Now my dear nameless fare whom I pick up each day   Fare = passenger
You'll hear many new tales as we go on our way.
We'll play many games with the noun and the verb
And the action goes on 'til we pull to the curb.

Like one day a criminal was robbing a bank
He was using a one-hundred-twenty-ton tank.   Ton = 2,000 pounds
The bees I had trained flew in a flurry
The man in the tank got out in a hurry
His hands in the air, his gun never tested
The law came around and the cad was arrested.   Cad = bad guy

And then there's the time that the church was afire
My butterfly carried me up to the spire.   Spire = steeple
I called forth my eagles who blocked out the sun
Their claws carried water, the job was soon done.
The people were spared in an orderly way   Orderly = neat
And Marceau, once again, had indeed saved the day.

These stories related are not rare events
They happen quite often and make very good sense.
I admit they're not fact but just how I feel
While driving my cab they appear very real.   Appear = seem
My adventures are laden with great joy and sorrow   Laden = filled
If you want to hear more … just tune in tomorrow.

Endangered Animals

Based on an original idea by Maxx & Gabe Fisher

Well, hello and good morning and how do you do
I have a sad, sad story of a poor, troubled zoo.

A frightening thing had occurred one night
It was a violent storm of incredible might.
A hurricane had struck New Orleans that day
And all of the people had run far away.
The zoo in the city was left unprotected
With all of the animals badly neglected.

Frightening = scary
Violent = strong, wild
Hurricane = huge wind

Neglected = uncared for

A torrential rain soon covered the zoo
The animals panicked, didn't know what to do.
Their nerves were frayed, their defenses heightened
They had every right to be very frightened.
It seems when the zoo had been almost forgotten
The animals' food had got wet and turned rotten
All had been locked up inside of their cages
And none had been out of those cages in ages.

Torrential = very heavy rain
Panicked = got scared
Frayed = ragged
Heightened = raised

Ages = a long time

I had very little time to be wasting that day–
I must get to the zoo the fastest way.

But the winds were so strong from the hurricane
That no one could fly in an airplane.
So strong were those winds, though it seemed quite absurd   Absurd = silly
It was not even safe on the wings of my bird.

It was silly to think about going by train
Since all of the bridges washed away in the rain.
The only way there was over the land
But not by the roads, which were covered with sand.

Then I thought of a cat whose tail is curled
The fastest animal in the entire world.
The fastest of the fastest is a feline named Rita
Who is known far and wide as the world's fastest cheetah.
She came when I called, just as quick as a wink
When I explained my dilemma, she started to think.   Dilemma = problem
"You can get on my back and we'll ride like the wind."
Then she tried to explain why she looked so chagrined.   Chagrined = unsure
"I can run only one hundred miles, I fear
But the zoo is one thousand miles from here.

It would be impossible," she said, "to achieve success
Unless we do it like they did it on the Pony Express."

Pony Express =
mail delivery

In the early days what we needed most
Was a way to get our mail from coast to coast.
The mail had to get through, it was a matter of pride
With the distance too great for just one man to ride.
It was a job for many, not just for one
So they kept changing horses 'til the journey was done.

What a really great idea, we might make it somehow
That's enough conversation. Let's get it done now.
It would require great effort to accomplish our ends
So Rita sure helped when she gathered her friends.
Nine other cheetahs would each do their part
Each would be waiting a hundred miles apart.

Conversation = talking
Accomplish = succeed

But getting to the zoo would be just the beginning
I'd need a lot of help to even think about winning.

Can you even imagine the problems involved?
There were mountains of problems that had to be solved.
Like when I finally get there, what will I do?
All of the animals need food, not just a few
Getting food to the hungry would be a great feat.
But as to half of those guys, I don't even know what they eat
Some of 'em need meat and some of 'em need hay

But whatever they eat, they need it today.

Preparations were begun, we were driven by pride
By the dawn of the day we had started our ride.
We traveled one hundred miles in less than two hours flat
I couldn't believe the great speed of that cat.
It all came together as anticipated   Anticipated = expected
For at every new station a fresh cheetah waited.
Through thickets and grasslands and rivers we breezed
Until we reached there next morning, quite tired but pleased.
Word was relayed by mysterious means
And from the corners of the earth came the rescue teams.
The elephants brought food that elephants eat
While the lions and tigers brought succulent meat.   Succulent = juicy
The eagles brought prey that they'd caught like a ball
And the camels brought plenty of water for all.
For the tiniest critters we furnished a ride
On the wings of the birds who came in with the tide.
To be helping an effort so noble, they thought   Noble = upstanding
Was a feeling of value that could not be bought.

Everyone ate, it was a sight to behold
Worth much more than bushels of diamonds and gold.
Before day was gone, we had fed quite a few
Like the wolf and the hippo and the kangaroo.
We fed egrets and polar bears, each white as vanilla
There were bananas galore for the amazing gorilla.
They brought branches for the timid, endangered okapi   Endangered = too rare
And food for the monkeys, who proved a bit sloppy
If you think that this journey had not been worthwhile
Ask the rhino or the zebra or the crocodile.
The giraffes had been fed and the chimpanzee, too
Happiness, at last, had returned to the zoo.

They cheered and they roared and created a din   Din = loud noise
So in view of the results, I'll just call it a win.
The waters receded, the keepers returned   Receded = went down
Never to forget the new lessons they learned.
From now on the food would be stored with great care
When next it was needed, it would surely be there.

Tomorrow's story, if you please
Is about a pirate that ruled the seas.
A pirate who says, "Arrgh" and calls me "Mate"
So I'll see you in the morning – try not to be late!

The Pirates

I am happy, dear sir, you could make it today
For I've quite a good story to tell on the way.
I'm sure if you listen quite closely you'll hear
An adventure tale full of intrigue and fear.   Intrigue = mystery

It seems on the briny a pirate did boast   Briny = ocean
Of how men from each village would wait on the coast.
And women and children, the young and the old
With their arms heavy laden by silver and gold.   Laden = loaded
He had threatened to burn down their village that night
And would kidnap the children if they put up a fight.   Kidnap = steal
This bounder, this Blackbeard, despicable man   Bounder = bad guy
Had destroyed the last town that had turned down his plan.
He gave an alternative that could save them the day   Alternative = choice
For the purchase of peace they would now have to pay.   Purchase = buy
Half of the treasures they kept in the town
There was little to do but be nice to this clown.

I conceived a design that I knew could not fail
And whistled for Gertrude, my favorite whale.
She came quick as a flash, as resilient as rubber
I'm tremendously fond of that large piece of blubber.
She was certainly pleased to be of assistance
And was bound to be met with just token resistance.
For the depth and the height and the breadth of this whale
Would cause even the meanest of villains to pale.

She swam 'neath the ship and she shook it quite soundly
Boy, I'd hate to be on it, I reasoned profoundly.
She'd shake from the frigate a pirate or two
She was doing precisely as ordered to do.
Marceau was now certain they'd pay for their crime
For the townsmen could handle one or two at a time.
We really must thank that adorable whale
For all of the bad guys are now sitting in jail.

It pleased you, I hope, for that's what was intended
We've arrived at your office, our journey is ended.
I have a tale for tomorrow that just waits to be told
About someone stealing something more precious than gold.
It's a really great story, one that made Marceau proud,
And he will tell you how it feels to ride on a cloud.

Conceived = thought of

Resilient = elastic
Tremendously = very
Assistance = help
Resistance = struggle
Token = least
Breadth = size
Pale = turn white
Soundly = a lot
Profoundly = deeply
Frigate = ship
Precisely = exactly

Intended = meant

15

The
Third Theft of the Mona Lisa

Based on an original idea by Jacob & Zachary Arrandt

Well, hello my dear friend, let me tell you a story
Of a mean, vicious man with no pride and no glory.   Vicious = very, very mean
The Louvre, in Paris, is a museum of fine art
And that's where this story had gotten its start.
It seems that the most famous painting of all
Had been stolen, one night, from its frame on the wall.
Leonardo da Vinci had been one heck of a guy
He was a marvelous artist; that, none could deny.
He had painted the *Mona Lisa* a long time ago
But today we still love it and bask in her glow.   Bask = relax and enjoy
Her smile is intriguing, her presence serene   Intriguing = interesting
She is possessed of an air that's befitting a queen.   Air = aura, glow
To have visited that painting was very worthwhile
For its beauty would cause one to pause and to smile.

The painting had been stolen once, twice, and then
Some very wicked people went and stole it again
Since this theft had been lacking both class and propriety   Propriety =
I assumed it was the dreaded Anti-Hedonistic Society.   good manners
Something scary once happened that made me afraid   Anti-Hedonistic=
Remind me to tell you of the Mardi Gras parade.   against fun

17

The same guys had attempted a terrible crime
But Marceau had been able to stop them that time.
Well, they're back once again with their old, evil style
Determined, as always, to stop everyone's smile.
It's the smile that they hated, their crusade had begun
Their goal was that none of us have any fun.
That's what they wanted, those terrible men
And they were up to their dirty old tricks once again.
These people, remember, were exceptionally mean
They wanted the painting to never be seen.

Crusade =
to achieve a goal

Exceptionally = very, very

In a fortress on a mountain, far, far away
The painting was hidden where they planned it would stay.
They wanted to hide it where no one could go
But they forgot about one thing; me, the amazing Marceau.

The police were befuddled, could not find a way
So Marceau was the answer, they decided that day
I was called and I went, as you all knew I would
To help solve this problem if only I could.

Befuddled = confused

Before I flew to that mountain in the middle of France
I considered which options would provide the best chance.
I thought of a plan that might even be fun
It was a way to make sure that the job would get done.
When I had visited the Grand Canyon in the U.S. of A.
I had seen a family of Big Horns there happily at play.

Options = choices

What's a Big Horn, you ask? A good question, my friend
Where do I begin, and where do I end?
Well, it's a sheep with big horns and the surest of feet
Who can run up a mountain without skipping a beat.
They are surprisingly strong, though they seem very fragile   Fragile = delicate
They are as fast as the wind and amazingly agile.   Agile = athletic
It's tough to believe how they scamper around
And they do it so quietly, hardly a sound.
Their movements are graceful, they run like the devil
They could run up a mountain as if it were level.

The boss of the bunch was a Big Horn named Sam
Who wore on his head a large battering ram.   Battering ram = big horns
Sam lived in the canyon and was always on call
He was able to run almost straight up a wall.
He could clear any path with little delay
I would never advise you to get in his way.
I asked that Sam join us. It was time we proceeded   Proceeded = started
The quickest way up was just what was needed.

So Sam and I swiftly got onto my bird
And we took off for France, where the crime had occurred.
It was time now to hurry, no time for a nap
Since the enemy was plotting and setting their trap.
The bad guys were ready, their plans had been made
Now let me review all the traps they had laid.

The mountain itself was as steep as a wall
And all who had climbed it were lost in a fall.
None had survived the hard climb to the peak   Peak = top
But none had attempted this brand-new technique.   Technique = method
The path we were on was just ten inches wide
But Sam proved to be an exceptional guide.   Exceptional = very, very good
Closer and closer and closer we came
This was serious business, not merely a game.
The bad guys, now desperate, showed us their wrath   Wrath = anger
By busting a gigantic hole in the path.
Sam just backed up and as calm as you please
Jumped over the hole with the greatest of ease.
Up, up we went with no thought to stop
Until at last he delivered me, safe at the top.

The ride up the mountain had been scary enough
When finally we got there, things really got rough.
When at last we had reached the top of the peak
We found it shrouded completely in hazy mystique.   Shrouded = masked
If you could have been there, you'd know what I mean   Hazy = fuzzy
You would never have believed that incredible scene.   Mystique = mystery
The fog parted briefly to vaguely reveal   Vaguely = not clearly
A veritable fortress of iron and steel.   Veritable = actual
It stood atop a glacier, in the middle of a lake   Glacier = island of ice
It would be difficult to get to, no room for mistake.
This was a problem of major proportions   Proportions = size
My mind went through a million contortions.   Contortion = strange position

There was no way to cross, it was too deep to ford

Ford = walk through

When a cloud drifted past me and bid me aboard.

This impossible problem was soon to be solved

When this cloud, named Marshmallow, got involved.

She was soft as a pillow, fluffy and white

For Marceau it was a case of love at first sight.

Did you ever imagine a ride on a cloud?

It was so much fun I was laughing out loud.

The cloud was like a coach so I sat down inside

Then we drifted 'cross the lake, how unique was my ride?

Unique =
one of a kind

Getting there had easily been half of the fun

But *Mona* was waiting, I really must run.

I gently alit when we came to a stop
Now I needed to reach the room at the top.
I ran up the stairs of that fortress so tall
And I came to a stop at the end of a hall.
I opened the door to a room with no label
And there lay the painting, alone on a table.
I reached for the object of all our desires
Hardly noticing that the table was covered with wires.
They had booby-trapped the painting, another of their games
I didn't know that if I touched it, it would go up in flames.

Alit = got off

Label = sign

Well, the fire flared fiercely, I grabbed *Mona*, however

Flared = burnt

It looked like the painting would be gone soon forever.
I was immediately relieved, I even said it aloud
When rain came pouring from that beautiful cloud.
Marshmallow descended and bade me to board

Descended = came down

I got on with *Mona* while the bad guys roared.

Bade = invited

They hollered and chased us, it was all very frightening
Until Marshmallow unleashed her great thunder and lightning.

Unleashed = released

Then it was over, as quick as a wink
The bad guys were blown way back into the drink.
Some of 'em surrendered but most ran away
Planning, I'm sure, to come back one day.
At last it was apparent Marceau would prevail

Prevail = succeed, win

And some of the crooks would be going to jail.

Who can we thank for this, who did us all proud?
It was a ram named Sam and a marshmallow cloud.

This tale was exciting, as anyone could see
There'll be another good one tomorrow, I'm sure you'll agree.

The Taming of the Tiger

Good morning, sir, greetings, we'll ride down in style
You'll agree, I am sure, that my tale is worthwhile.
So be at ease, my good man, and set your mind free
And I'll tell you what recently happened to me.

There's a small town in India where some people got mad
Because their school had to close and the children were sad.
They were eager to study things like science and math
But a gigantic tiger was blocking the path.   Gigantic = really big
He had no need to be there, he was just being mean
So Marceau was then asked, would he please intervene.   Intervene = step in

A message was sent on a great eagle's wings
I got it, I nodded, and I gathered my things.
Marceau asks not where, Marceau asks not why
I mounted Majesty, the eagle, and flew to the sky.   Mounted = got on
I peered through the clouds from my seat on the bird   Peered = looked
And prepared for the problem to which I referred.   Prepared = got ready
We set down some distance from where we began
And again I would prove that Marceau was a man.

As I walked to the school through the jungle that day
The tiger they spoke of was blocking my way.
He was muscled and striped and he weighed half a ton
And his teeth glistened meanly when caught by the sun.   Glisten = shine
I asked him to move in a most mannerly way   Mannerly = polite
But from all indications he intended to stay.   Indications = hints

My predicament demanded I now take a chance   Predicament = problem
So I looked all around me for some kind of lance.   Lance = spear
There were none to be seen, my mind in a flurry
No time for reflection, I knew I must hurry.   Reflection = thinking

The beast rushed right past me as I stepped aside
My leg swung up quickly 'til I was astride.   Astride = mounted
He raced like a rabbit, not liking the weight
But he messed with Marceau and this was his fate.   Fate = future
He spun on the ground and he banged into trees
He leapt high on branches, he fell to his knees.   Leapt = jumped
He rolled in the water, his efforts a flop
Whatever maneuver, Marceau was on top.   Maneuver = movement

The great tiger's power became less confusing
I was beginning to think it all very amusing.
I laughed as I rode him, one hand in the air
Like a cowboy I saw at an old county fair.
One hand gripped tightly the skin on his back
As I rode that old tiger all over the track.

The crowd roared approval, the job please don't bungle!
How did they get such a crowd in the jungle?

Bungle = mess up

The ride was tremendous, my styling was grand
And even the tiger was shaking my hand.
The cat was so sorry he said it aloud
I flew off on the eagle as I waved to the crowd.

Grand = classy

Once again I'd accomplished a deed clean and pure
I was leaving the jungle completely secure.
Trouble had threatened, the job had been done
And as all had expected, Marceau was the one.
Marceau wins most battles, at least ten out of ten
To hear yet another, please come back again.

Accomplished = finished
Secure = safe

The Beautiful Princess

Based upon conversations with my personal princesses, Jessica and Sloan Fisher

The traffic was heavy, I'm sorry I'm late
But my story today will be well worth the wait.
It's a tale of a crime that just had to be solved
And there's a very, very beautiful Princess involved.

When did this happen? It was "once upon a time"
That Marceau had been called on to help solve the crime.
This is a story of courage, of love and of winning   Courage = bravery
But first things first, let's begin at the beginning.
It's the tale of a beautiful, magical crown
That from king to king had been handed on down.
That fabulous crown, adorned with great worth   Adorned = decorated
Was made of diamonds and rubies, the finest on earth.
There were emeralds and opals, the treasures of kings
And platinum and pearls and a few other things.
It was the most beautiful crown that had ever been seen
And would belong to the Princess when she became queen.

The King was her father, a very powerful man
Who had hopes that the future would follow his plan.

And his plan for the Princess was noble, indeed — Noble = good
That she be happy and healthy and in all things succeed
So he told her his wishes and caveats, too. — Caveats = warnings
"Do not let this crown get too far from you
For if you should lose it, whatever the cause
You will not be the queen, and that's simply because
With the crown goes the power, the strength and the magic — Tragic = horrible
Without it the consequences are bound to be tragic. — Consequences = results
"So be careful, my child, please take care of this thing–
Without it, even I would cease to be king. — Cease = stop
I'm trusting this treasure, it is now in your care
If you lose it your queendom will never be there.
Your sister, Elvina, will then get the crown
She'll be the queen and can boss you around."

Now the Princess Elvina was ugly and mean
It would be a terrible thing if she became queen.
She had long red hair and a big wart on her nose
And always wore the shabbiest, dirtiest clothes. — Shabbiest = torn
If the Princess's little sister ever got to be queen
The first chance she had, she would get really mean.
She would tax and oppress all the citizens there — Oppress = treat badly
And if they were hungry and tired, she just wouldn't care
As long as she had all the things she could want — Preen = pose
She would preen and be boastful and act nonchalant. — Boastful = bragging
But soon she'd want more and would start to be bad — Nonchalant = relaxed
Then life in the kingdom would be sad, very sad.

There'd be no money for candy, that wouldn't be cool
And the bad queen might even shut down the school.
That's a horrible thought and it caused great concern
'Cause there'd be no place to play and no place to learn.

Concern = worry

But the beautiful Princess wished to do only good
And to show the crown to the world, if only she could.
She was so sweet and so kind and she helped feed the poor
She'd make a wonderful queen, that's one thing for sure.
She would share the crown's beauty, if only they'd let her
Then everyone who saw it would start to feel better.
It would fill the world with beauty and fill it with romance
So the Princess decided she would take a small chance.

The crown, we all know, would be much less secure

Secure = safe

Yet she foolishly decided that she would take it on tour.
She was welcomed by flags that flew high above her
All the people, you see, had now grown to love her.
The Princess said, "Mayor, your town is so pretty."
The mayor said, "I hope you feel safe in our city."
"I feel very safe," was the Princess's reply.
"But I'd feel even safer if Marceau was nearby."
"Nothing must go wrong, there is too much at stake

At stake = to lose

We must always be vigilant, alert and awake."

Vigilant = watchful

Since she required the assistance Marceau could provide

Assistance = help

I volunteered my services to act as her guide.

35

If anything bad happens it would be a great pity
With that on our minds we began our tour of the city.
People cheered as she passed in her pretty pink gown
And they "oohed" and they "aahed" when they looked at the crown.
It was the most beautiful crown that they ever had seen
And they agreed it belonged on the head of this queen.
Marceau led the way, she walked very close behind me
Then something bad happened, there's no need to remind me.

We had been walking for a while but when I next looked around
The Princess was missing and so was her crown.
I spun on my heels, I looked in every direction
Whatever just happened had escaped my detection.   Detection = discovery
So where was the Princess, and where was the crown?
The entire police force was searching the town
A group of tall buildings surrounded the square
And I thought that the Princess would surely be there.

I returned to the spot from where she had been taken
On a hunch I looked up and I was not mistaken.
There was someone on the roof in a hooded disguise
He was holding the Princess, who had tears in her eyes.
It was scary to watch them way out on the ledge
As he threatened to push her clear over the edge.

I let out a loud whistle, I put everything in it
My eagle responded in less than a minute.   Responded = answered

I mounted the eagle, made plans to attack   Mounted = got on
But the cad had a plan and it made me hold back.   Cad = bad guy
He dangled the Princess by the tip of her toe
Who knows what would happen if he should let go?
Well, he did let her drop, that horrible man
Then he picked up the crown and he ran and he ran.
When she could no longer hold on by her fingertips
A frightening scream came away from her lips.

Now I must quickly decide, should we chase after him?
Or rescue the Princess, whose future looked grim?   Grim = bad
She was falling so quickly, her skirts all awhirl
I am sure that you guessed we went after the girl.
Head over heels she fell toward the ground
It was lucky, indeed, that Marceau was around.
Down, down she tumbled, it seemed like the end
But the bad guy forgot that Marceau was her friend.
With the grace of an eagle, Majesty swooped down   Grace = beauty
Gently caught her and brought her to rest on the ground.

She was pleased as could be that her life had been spared
But the crown was now missing and the Princess was scared.
Her eyes filled with tears, her cheeks all aglow
"We can't let this happen," she cried to Marceau.

There were rivers and valleys and forests and peaks
Searching would surely take too many weeks.

That was way too much time for our plan to allow
We needed the crown and we needed it now.
Majesty cawed loudly as she put out the word
And her message was relayed from bird to bird.   Relayed = one to another
Soon thirty-seven eagles flew in to our aid
And in the blink of an eye our plan had been made.
Have you heard the expression, "an eagle eye"?   Expression = saying
Well, the eagles spread out and they covered the sky
In just a few minutes that title was earned
For the bad guy had been spotted, caught and returned.

Who was this bad guy that had filled us with dread?   Dread = fear
The hood that he wore still covered his head
When I pulled off the hood, long, red hair tumbled down
It was Elvina, herself, who had stolen the crown.
Guilty she was, we had caught her redhanded
"Bring her to me," the King then commanded.
The King raised some questions about the assault   Assault = attack
He wished to discover who was really at fault.

We all knew Elvina had lied when she spoke
She was trying to explain, "It was only a joke."
Everyone knew better, what else can I say?
After all, my good friend, we weren't born yesterday.
He listened as his daughter tried to be cool
But he proved to Marceau that he was nobody's fool.
The King, in his anger, had something to say
He banished Elvina to a land far away.   Banished = sent away
She would never return, for that was his plan
Then the people rejoiced and the parties began.   Rejoiced = were happy
There was joy in the land, the air filled with laughter
Then everyone there lived happily ever after…

That's all for now but look to the sky
You can see Marceau on the eagle, waving good-bye.
It's been a week of excitement, I'm sure you'll agree
And the action will continue in Week Number Three!

About the author

JOE BROWN lives in the village of Lincolnwood, Illinois, with his wife, Lola. He was an attorney in Chicago for fifty years before embarking on a writing career at age 70. Bop, as he is known in the family, started writing these stories for his children in the 1960s. After retiring he began, again, writing about Marceau's adventures. This is the second book of an ongoing series that has taken more than forty years to write.

About the artists

MICHAEL PUKÁČ was born and raised on the Gulf coast of Alabama and now resides in Sarasota, Florida, where he graduated from the Ringling School of Art. His illustrations are done in acrylics and clearly reflect his fine art skills.

STEPHEN MARCHESI has illustrated numerous picture books, textbooks and magazines. A graduate of Pratt Institute, his

books have been on the Children's Book Council best-sellers list and on the Bank Street College Children's Book of the Year lists. He lives with his wife and son in Croton-on-Hudson, New York.